The
MAGIC
STONES

The Gnomes

By Debbie S Blankenship

Illustrated by Cris Davis Hart

This book is dedicated to my family.

Jeremiah 1:5 says: "Before I formed you in the womb I knew you, before you were born, I set you apart..."

Always remember that you were born on purpose, for a purpose. Jeremiah 29:11 says: "For I know the plans I have for you," declares the LORD, "plans to prosper you and not to harm you, plans to give you hope and a future."

Proverbs 18:21 says: "The tongue has the power of life and death, and those who love it will eat its fruit." Speak life to yourself and to others. You are LOVED! Don't say, "I'm so stupid," or "I can't remember anything," or "I'm too ugly."

Believe what God says about you, and do not let your tongue destroy you with words of self-loathing. Speak God's truth to yourself and those you love, not the enemy's lies. Jesus says, "You are worth dying for!" You are on His mind all the time. The Holy Spirit lives inside everyone who accepts Jesus as their savior, so He is with you, always. If it seems the door to your dreams closes, look for the door that God will open for an even better dream!

When I became a Christian, I learned this song:
"This world is not my home,
I'm just passing through,
My treasures are laid out,
Somewhere beyond the blue,
His angels beckon me,
From heaven's open door,
And I can't feel at home,
In this world anymore."
Make sure that Heaven is YOUR home.
I love you all.

Contents

CHAPTER 1
The New School

The boys were sad that the summer was over and felt a little nervous about starting in a new school. They had spent the summer with their cousins, exploring the acres of woods around their new house.

"Owen!" Mom hollered up the stairs. "We have to leave in five minutes! If you're going to eat you better get down here!"

Owen was still up in his bedroom putting his shoes on. He grabbed his backpack and slowly walked down the stairs into the kitchen. His brothers, Max and Brody, were already finished eating and were throwing a small ball to each other over the table.

"Watch it!" Owen growled, as the ball narrowly missed his head.

"Take that ball out of here and get your teeth brushed," Mom instructed. "Owen, your toast is on the table, you'd better hurry."

He sat down and started to eat. "I don't want to go to school," he pouted. "I don't know anyone in my class."

"I know it's hard to go to a new school, but you will make friends quickly," Mom told him, trying to relieve some of his fears.

Owen finished his toast and went to brush his teeth. Then they all grabbed their backpacks and headed to the car.

"Did you decide to try out for the baseball team?" asked Mom as they drove to the school.

"Maybe," Owen answered.

"It would be a good way to make some friends," Mom encouraged.

"I guess I will," Owen agreed.

When they got to the drop-off point the boys gathered their backpacks and the principal, Mr. Swingler, opened the van door. They had met him the night of orientation and he remembered their names.

"Hello Owen, Max and Brody!" he greeted. "Nice to see you again Mrs. Daniels. We'll take good care of them."

"Nice to see you again, Mr. Swingler," she answered. "Pick up is at three?"

"Yes," he responded, then walked with the boys to the door. "You all remember where your classes are?"

"I think so," answered Brody.

"The junior high wing is through those doors?" Owen asked him.

"That's right," he answered.

"I know where to go from here," Owen assured him.

Owen started to go through the double doors, then turned to his brothers, "Your class is just down that hallway."

"We know," they both answered, and walked away. Owen watched them go for a minute, then went through the doors. He went down the long hallway that housed the lockers, looking for his. He had found it on school orientation day, so knew about where it was.

"Number 13," he said out loud as he stopped.

"Number 12," said a blond boy, stopping next to him.

Owen looked at him. He was about Owen's height with curly hair. He had a friendly smile and said, "Hi, I'm Conner. You must be the new kid that moved into that old house on Iron Gate. Is it haunted like everyone says?"

Owen laughed, "I don't think so. I'm Owen Daniels."

Conner put his hand out and Owen shook it. "Who do you have for homeroom?"

Owen pulled his schedule out, "Mrs. Rinella."

"Me too! I'll show you where it is." Conner offered. "Do you play ball? Are you going to try out for the team tonight?"

"Yes, are you?" asked Owen.

"Yup," Conner answered as they walked into their classroom.

Mrs. Rinella had everyone sit down and started taking roll. When she got to Owen's name she paused.

"Mr. Daniels, welcome to our homeroom!" She said. "Why don't you stand up and tell us a little bit about yourself."

Owen looked around the room and stood, "I'm Owen Daniels, and we just moved here over the summer."

"Tell us about your family," Mrs. Rinella encouraged, "do you have any brothers or sisters?"

"I have two brothers," Owen informed her, "Max and Brody. They are twins, but not identical."

"Are they in school?" she continued.

"Yes, they are in 4th grade." Owen answered.

"I look forward to meeting them!" Mrs. Rinella said. "You may sit down now."

Owen sat back in his seat, feeling a little self-conscious.

Max and Brody walked into their class. All the kids stopped and stared at them as they found two desks to sit at. The bell rang and they turned their attention to the teacher standing before them. She walked to the dry erase board and printed her name, Mrs. Goodson.

"Good morning class," she cheerfully started. "Who else, beside me, is ready to start a new school year?"

The class moaned a little.

Laughing aloud, she continued, "We are going to have so much fun, and learn lots of new, exciting things. First let's welcome our two new students, Max and Brody Daniels."

The class said their obligatory hellos.

"Come up to the front," Mrs. Goodson directed them.

Max and Brody looked at each other, feeling awkward, then slowly got up and walked to the teacher.

"Tell us a little bit about yourselves," she said.

They both shrugged, not knowing what to say.

"Where are you from?" she prompted.

"Oshkosh," Brody answered.

"And what brought you to Greenville?" she continued.

"Our Aunt Barbie gave us her old house, and our cousins live here," answered Max.

"Camden Daniels is your cousin? I had him as a student last year," she told them.

They nodded yes.

"Is your house really haunted?" one of the students hollered out.

Mrs. Goodson laughed a little, "Bryce is referring to the old tale about your house being haunted by some kind of creatures."

Max and Brody looked at each other again. Had someone else seen Jack and his family?

"We haven't seen anything," Brody said. "It's just a regular house."

"Those old tales about strange creatures in the woods are just that, old tales told by people with too much imagination," Mrs. Goodson said to the class. "Welcome to our class Max and Brody, you may take your seats."

They sat down, smiling a little at each other as they thought about Jack the sasquatch.

At recess Bryce came over to them. "Hi! I'm Bryce. These are my friends, Connell and Carsten."

"Are you sure there are no creatures in the woods by your house?" Carsten asked.

"The teacher told you it is just an old tale!" Bryce scoffed.

Max and Brody nodded in agreement with Bryce, then changed the subject. "Want to shoot some baskets?" Max suggested.

"We can play 'horse'!" Bryce agreed, and they ran over to the basketball court.

When the bell rang the kids lined up to go back into the building. Mrs. Rinella was at the door and when she saw Max and Brody she walked up to them, "You must be Owen's twin brothers."

They nodded.

"Let me see if I can remember your names." After a few seconds she guessed, "You must be Mac," she said pointing at Max, "and you must be..." she paused a second more, "Wac?" she asked, looking at Brody. Both boys laughed. "Was I close?" Mrs. Rinella asked, smiling.

"Not really," Max told her. "I'm Max."

"And I'm Brody," Brody informed her.

Laughing, Mrs. Rinella said, "I'll try to remember, but I think I like Mac and Wac. It has a nice ring to it!" she teased.

Kristy was there to pick up Max and Brody at 3 o'clock, then they walked over to the junior high baseball field to wait for Owen. He waved at his mother and brothers when he saw them sitting in the stands and ran his backpack over to them, then ran back to the dugout.

"How was your first day at school?" Kristy asked Max.

"Good," he answered.

"That's it? Just good?" she chuckled. "How about you Brody?"

"It was good," he agreed.

Kristy laughed, "Did you meet some new friends? Did you like your teacher?"

"Yeah," Brody answered, "we met a boy named Bryce, he was cool."

"And Connell," Max added.

"Did you know everyone thinks our house is haunted?" Brody asked.

"They do?" She responded, looking surprised.

"Yes!" replied Max. "The teacher told them it was just an old tale."

"I heard the story about a black, hairy thing living in the woods," Kristy confessed, "but never that the house was haunted." She looked at both boys. "You don't believe it, do you? That our house is haunted?"

"No," they both said. "Our house is cool!" Max added, looking at Brody, who nodded in agreement.

Owen was listening to the coach give instructions. He divided the kids into two groups and had them play a couple of innings against each other. "Owen Daniels, you're in right field," he said. Owen grabbed his glove and ran onto the field. A boy named Easton was sent to center field. Conner, the boy whose locker was next to Owens, was first at bat. On the first pitch he hit a fly ball straight to Easton in center field and he caught it easily.

"Nice catch!" Owen yelled at him.

The next batter hit a ball down the first base line where a boy named Harper was playing. He scooped it up and touched the bag.

The next batter, a boy named Jackson, hit a hard grounder to right field. Owen charged the ball and threw him out at first.

They continued to play until everyone hit, then switched. As Owen waited his turn at bat, Harper, the boy who played first base, said, "That was a good throw."

"Thanks," Owen responded.

"Harper!" the coach barked, "you are on deck! Owen, you're in the hole."

They both grabbed their helmets and got in position. When Harper got up to bat the outfielders all backed up. He was a big boy, a head taller than most of the kids trying out. He swung at the first pitch and missed. The second pitch was too low, so he let it go by. The third pitch looked good, so he swung hard, hitting the ball, sending it sailing over the heads of the outfielders. He made it to second base easily.

Owen was a little nervous as he went up to bat. The first pitch was inside, and he let it go by. The second pitch was called a strike, even though Owen didn't think it was. He took a practice swing and waited for the pitch. It looked good coming in, and he swung. It sailed into the outfield just out of reach of the left fielder, and he made it safely to first. The next batter hit a hard grounder between first and second base and Owen took off running. He knew it was going to be close as he slid into second base. The throw from the outfield was wild and the second baseman couldn't catch it, so he was safe. He could hear his mom and brothers cheering from the stands. The last batter hit a fly ball that was caught by the center fielder and the coach called them all in. "I'll post the roster in a few days and then we will start practice next week," he informed.

On the ride home Kristy asked Owen, "Did you meet some new friends?"

"A boy named Conner is in a few of my classes. He was nice, and he tried out for baseball too," Owen told her.

As they pulled into the driveway she said, "I made everyone's favorite for supper, beef and noodles!"

"I'm starving!" Max announced and ran into the house.

CHAPTER 2
Lilly

That evening Mom said that she had a surprise. "Your father is going to be home next week!" The boys were very excited. Their Dad had been on a special assignment all summer. He was part of a Seal Team, and they were never exactly sure where he was when he was gone. "I want to get the house cleaned up for him," she continued. "This weekend you three are going to help by raking the leaves and pulling some weeds."

"Yeah, Dad has never seen this house," Owen agreed. "We need to clean it up, so he has time to get the zipline installed!" Adam had promised to put one up for them when he got home.

When Saturday morning came, Kristy woke the kids up early. "I'm fixing eggs and pancakes for breakfast, so we will all have plenty of energy to get things done. Get your play clothes on and come down to eat." When they were all at the table she told them, "Kari and your cousins are going to come over to help."

"Is Uncle Austin coming home too?" Max asked. Austin was Adam's brother, and they were both on the same Seal Team.

"Yes," Mom answered. "They will be on the same plane."

Just then Kari came through the door. "We brought donuts!" she announced, walking into the kitchen.

Camden and Reaghan sat down at the table and Kristy said, "Ooooo, those look good! Do you want some eggs and pancakes too?"

As the kids picked out their favorite donut Kari got plates out. "Camden, do you want eggs or pancakes?"

"No, I'll just have a donut," he answered.

"Reaghan?" Kari asked.

"A pancake please," she told her Mom.

When the kids were taken care of, Kari sat down and laughed, "I see you are having your usual bowl of cereal. Do you ever eat anything else?"

Kristy chuckled, "No, I like cereal!"

When everyone was done eating, Kari asked, "Where do you want us to start?"

"I have rakes and wheelbarrows ready outside for the kids to work in the yard," Kristy answered. "And you and I are going to tackle the den, where I still have unpacked boxes. If we have time I would like to paint in there also."

Owen said, "Ok, let's get started," and all the kids went out the door. They found the supplies Kristy had put in the backyard. Owen and Camden grabbed a rake as she came out the door.

"I want you to wheelbarrow the leaves over to the burn pile in the back," she instructed. "Also, see if you can drag some of those big branches that fell in the yard over there too. If they are too heavy don't worry about them, we can leave those for Dad when he gets home."

"Ok, Mom." Max answered. The kids got busy raking and Kristy went back in the house.

"This would be easier if we go get the stones," Camden whispered to Max.

"We should!" Max agreed. "Owen, let's go get the stones out of the basement."

Owen looked around, like he was checking to see if anyone was watching them. "I guess we could, but we need to be careful."

"There's nobody out here but us," Brody assured. "And Mom and Aunt Kari are going to be busy on the other side of the house."

"Let's do it," Reaghan said in an excited tone.

They all agreed and went back into the house. As they were headed to the basement, and the secret room, Kristy came around the corner. "What's the matter?" she asked.

"N-Nothing!" sputtered Max. "We were just..." He looked at the others for help.

"We were just going to look in the basement f-for..." Reaghan stammered, then looked at Camden.

"Gloves!" Owen shouted. "We thought we saw some in a box down there." The others nodded in agreement.

"Ok," Kristy said, "but don't get distracted down there. You have a lot of work to do."

"We won't!" they responded in unison and scrambled down the stairs.

Everyone went straight to the back of the basement where the secret door hid.

"Every time we open this it feels like the first time," Brody whispered. He went to the box they had hidden the keys in and retrieved them. They all grabbed the shelf that stood in front of the secret door and slid it out of the way.

As Brody unlocked it Max said, "I still don't know why we can't just keep the stones with us."

"We all agreed that it would be too risky to have them while we are at school," Owen reminded him.

"I know," Max answered, "but I think we can all control our special powers."

"You wouldn't be tempted to outrun everyone in gym?" Owen asked sarcastically.

Max just glared at him. "No more than you would be tempted to get the right answers from your teacher's thoughts!"

"Exactly!" Owen agreed. "That's why they stay in here."

The door was open, and Camden flipped on the light switch. They walked over to the small chest and Brody unlocked it. He took the small, velvet bag out and poured the stones onto the floor.

"Hello Pinky!" Reaghan said with a smile.

"Pinky?" Max questioned. "You named your stone?"

"I did!" Reaghan stated, and they all laughed.

Each child was careful to pick up the right color stone. They knew the special powers that each of them was given would not work if they didn't. The magic stones began to glow in their hands and they each could feel the power of the stone pulsing through their bodies. Owen pulled out the small pouches they had purchased to carry the stones around their necks and handed one to each child. Smiling at the others he said, "Let's get to work!"

They were careful to close the room and put the shelf back, which Camden easily picked up and moved. He had received the power of super strength.

They went back outside and started working and couldn't help but let their powers out for a minute. Reaghan was near the woods, cleaning up the small branches, and Owen watched her as she let her ninja powers take over, flipping and twisting in the air, then scooping up a branch, landing with the agility of a cat.

Max was manning the wheelbarrow and decided to use his super speed to empty the leaves on the burn pile, however, he went so fast that all the leaves blew out and when he stopped to dump it on the pile there were no leaves left. He grinned at Owen and Camden who were raking. "I don't want to keep raking the same leaves up, Max," Camden growled. "Slow down!"

Brody had been standing near the house, examining something in the landscaping. "Are you just going to stand there, or are you going to help?" Owen hollered.

"Come here," Brody answered.

"What, do you see another spider web?" Owen mocked.

"No, seriously, come here!" Brody insisted. "I've never seen tracks like this before."

"How can you see tracks in the rocks?" Camden questioned as they all walked over to look.

"Something was moving around over here, and it wasn't a squirrel, or racoon," Brody told them. He slowly followed the trail to a large bush, then froze.

"Are you sure?" Owen asked him excitedly.

"What?!" Camden implored. "We can't read your mind like Owen. Tell us!"

"There is something in this bush," Brody answered softly.

All the children gathered around, trying to see into the thick bush.

"Owen," Max asked, "can you read it's mind?"

"No, but I can feel it's fear," he replied. "I'll see if I can let it know that we won't hurt it." They all remained quiet as Owen tried to communicate with it.

"Well?" asked Reaghan after a few minutes, "Did you talk to it?"

"Sort of," Owen said. "I think it is stuck in there."

"What should we do?" Brody asked.

"You and I can try to get closer," Owen instructed. "Everyone else stay back so it doesn't feel threatened."

Brody and Owen knelt by the base of the bush, but it was so thick they couldn't see into it. "Max," Owen said softly, "go look in the garage for the bush trimmer and bring it here."

Max disappeared instantly, using his super speed, and was back in a matter of seconds. "Sorry it took me so long," he gasped, trying to catch his breath, "I had a hard time finding it."

Camden chuckled as he took the trimmer from his hand and gave it to Brody. "Yeah, what took you so long?"

Brody slowly started to trim away some of the branches, making sure he did not get too close to the creature. He stopped suddenly, peering into the bush.

"Wow," Owen whispered, as he 'saw' what Brody was looking at in his mind.

"What is it?" asked Camden.

"I'm not sure," Brody answered. "I've never seen anything like it."

"What does it look like?" Reaghan questioned.

As Brody studied it, Owen tried to describe it to the others. "It's small, with long white hair, and kind of looks like a tiny doll."

"A doll?" asked Reaghan. "Can I look?" She walked over to the bush and bent down. Brody started to object, thinking she might scare it, when Owen said, "Let her look, it seems to like her." He got out of the way, and she stuck her head into the bush. Pulling her head back out she told them, "It's caught in some kind of string."

"Fishing wire," Brody clarified.

"I need a small scissors," Reaghan insisted, "I think I can cut it loose."

Max ran back to the garage and found some, then zoomed back to the bush. "Here you go," he puffed, handing them to her.

Reaghan slowly made her way under the bush, until her head and shoulders were no longer visible to the boys. She began talking to the creature, "Oh, my! You really are tangled!" They could hear the snip, snip of the scissors as she worked to free it. "Hold still little one, I almost have it." A few more snips and she began backing out of the bush.

The boys got their first look at the small thing. "Wow," commented Max, "It looks more like my stuffed bear than a doll."

It had long hair that covered all its body except the face. The hair there was much shorter, and revealed large, dark eyes. Its face was almost the shape of a cat's face, with big ears that would lay back nearly flat on its head at times. It had small, human-like hands and feet, except at the end of each finger and toe was a sharp, curved claw. It was still very tangled in the fishing line and Reaghan held it in her lap as she continued to try to free it. "I have to cut away some of its hair to get the string off," she told the others as she continued. By the time she had all the line off it there was nearly no hair left.

"The thing almost looks bald now," Owen noticed.

"I'm so sorry little one!" Reaghan apologized, petting it gently. The morning was chilly, and the little creature began to shiver. "Camden!" Reaghan called, "go to mom's car and see if my old doll is still in the back seat, then bring it here."

"It's not a good time to play dolls right now," he growled at her.

"Just go get it!" she insisted. "I have an idea."

Camden shrugged at the others and walked over to the car, retrieving the doll from the back. "Here you go," he said holding out the doll.

"Undress it," she instructed.

"What? Why?" he argued.

Brody took the doll from him, "I think I know why," and took the flannel dress off the doll, giving it to her.

"This will keep you warm until your hair grows back," Reaghan said softly as she slowly put it over the creature's head.

"I can't believe it's letting you do that!" Camden observed, as the thing cooperated.

Once it was dressed, it sat quietly, looking at each child. When it looked at Owen, it held its hand out to him.

"It wants to touch you," Reaghan told him.

Owen bent down and put his hand out. The creature took a hold of his finger, looking him straight in the eyes. They sat like that for several minutes, then it let go.

"What did it say?" Reaghan asked.

"It is grateful for our help," Owen said. "Their kind have been in these woods for centuries. They live in the trees."

Brody started looking up in the treetops, "I wonder why I never saw them?"

Owen chuckled, "I'll show you why." He started walking to the woods, "Reaghan, bring it here." She carried it over to the edge of the trees where Owen had stopped. It suddenly got very squirmy and leapt out of her hands. It was very fast for its size and scurried to a large tree. Brody was waiting for it to climb, but it simply disappeared around the base. Walking behind the tree, Brody realized why. The base of the tree had a small hollow. "They live in the tree hollows?" he asked.

"Yes, but it's better than that," Owen told him. "There is a weave of tunnels in the woods, and they connect to ´all the trees with hollows. They rarely need to move out in the open, which is why we have never encountered them before."

"What is it, did it tell you?" asked Max.

"It was something like Gonomies," Owen answered, "I'm not sure that is right though."

Just then Kristy called out the back door, "How is it going? Are you almost finished?"

"Almost, Mom!" Owen hollered back. "Just a few more minutes!" Then, looking at the others he said, "We better get busy, or she will wonder what we have been doing out here."

Everyone got back to cleaning the yard and they had it finished 30 minutes later, thanks to some special powers. When they went in the house Kristy said, "Take off your shoes at the door, then go upstairs and get cleaned up for lunch."

As they were waiting to wash their hands, they softly discussed their new friend. "Do you think we will ever see her again?" Reaghan asked.

"Was it a girl?" Camden asked Owen.

He thought for a moment then said, "I'm not sure."

"We should give her a name," Reaghan suggested.

"Furry!" suggested Max.

"No!" Reaghan vetoed the suggestion. "How about Lilly?"

"Why Lilly?" Camden asked.

"Because that was my doll's name that I took the dress off of," Reaghan answered.

"It's fine with me," Owen agreed. The rest of the boys just shrugged.

"I was thinking," Reaghan continued, "maybe we should keep the stones with us, just in case Lilly or her friends should need us."

"We all agreed that we were not going to take them to school," reminded Camden.

"She has a point," Brody added. "What if one of them got in some more trouble?"

"It could be risky," Owen warned. "What if the whole school found out about our powers?"

"We'll make sure that doesn't happen," promised Max.

Owen looked at everyone, "Ok, let's try it!"

"Great!" Reaghan grinned. "Owen, you'll have to let me know if you sense any danger for Lilly or her family."

"I will," he promised.

Just then Kari hollered up the stairs, "Are you done washing up? Lunch is ready."

"We're done!" they yelled back and hurried down the stairs.

CHAPTER 3

Gnomes Are Real?

S unday morning, after church, Kari and the kids
went back to Kristy's to finish the den.

She picked up some pizza on the way and Kristy
made a salad for lunch. Reaghan had brought her small
backpack in with her and when the kids were done eating,
she said, "Let's go outside and play." She picked up her
pack and the boys followed her outside.

"What do you have in there?" Camden asked her.

"I have an idea," she answered, and walked to the tree
that Lilly had disappeared in. Then she opened her backpack and dumped out the contents.

"Doll clothes?" Max questioned.

"Owen, can you send Lilly a message to come here?"
she asked.

"I can try," he told her, and put his hand on the tree
trunk, trying to communicate with the creature. After a
minute he took his hand off the tree and said, "I'm not sure
she got the message."

"Are you going to change its clothes?" Brody asked.

"She is not an IT!" Reaghan corrected, "and I'm going to see if she wants any of these."

"Oh brother," grumbled Camden.

"It is going to take some time to grow her hair back!" Reaghan retorted, adding, "No one wants to wear the same thing every day!"

"Max wears the same underwear every day!" Owen teased, then ran, knowing Max would be after him. Max easily caught him, and they started wrestling.

"You should know you can't run from Max," Camden laughed. He picked up a stick from the burn pile and pretended to duel with Brody, who also grabbed a stick. Pretty soon all the kids had sticks and were pretending to be pirates, playing on the edge of the woods.

After a few minutes Reaghan noticed that all the clothes she had left by the tree were gone. "She came and got them!" she announced excitedly.

They all went back to the tree with the hollow.

"I had hoped to see Lilly again," Reaghan said sadly.

"Now she won't have to be embarrassed wearing the same clothes," Camden kidded.

"She'll be nice and warm this winter, thanks to you," Brody said to Reaghan, trying to make her feel better.

Just then a little head popped out of the tree. Reaghan knelt and held her hand out. "Hi Lilly," she said softly.

The small creature came out and walked to her hand.

"She changed her clothes already!" Brody observed.

"I told you so!" Reaghan gloated. Lilly climbed into her arms and Reaghan cradled her in the crook of her elbow. Then Lilly made a shrill, bird like sound and pointed towards the hollow in the tree. The children stared in amazement as more of the small creatures slowly emerged, all of them now wearing one of the doll's outfits.

"Unbelievable!" whispered Max.

The boys knelt down, holding their hands out, inviting the things to come closer, and to their amazement, they did! Each child was able to touch the curious little creatures.

"Is this your family?" Reaghan asked Lilly, as if she expected her to talk back.

"I think it is," Owen answered, then looking back at the house he said "Uh-oh!"

Just then Kari and Kristy came out the back door.

"We have to leave soon," Kari called to Camden and Reaghan.

Kristy added, "Everyone come back into the house."

The children had all frozen, hoping they didn't see the small creatures surrounding them. The odd thing was that the creatures had also frozen in place, looking like small statues.

"We're coming!" Camden hollered back.

As the two moms went back into the house the creatures moved quickly back into the tree.

"Do you think Mom saw them?" Reaghan asked worriedly, watching Lilly disappear into the tree.

"They don't seem alarmed, so maybe not?" Owen said, as he tried to read their thoughts.

When the children got back in the house Kristy said, "I made some hot chocolate if you want some."

"Yes!" they answered and sat at the table by the cups she had already poured.

"What were you doing out there?" Kari asked.

"Just playing," Camden said, glancing at the others.

As the kids all took a sip of their cocoa Kristy asked, "Where did you find all those Gnomes?"

Each child spewed the cocoa out of their mouths.

"Is it too hot?" Kristy asked, chuckling.

"Yeah, that's it," Owen agreed, as he mopped up his mess with a napkin.

"Were they in the garage?" Kristy asked again.

"What?" Brody questioned.

"Those garden Gnomes," Kristy clarified.

"Um, y-yes, we found them in the garage," Owen stuttered.

"Maybe you can use those in your landscaping," Kari suggested.

The kids stared at each other. "They weren't in very good shape," Brody informed.

"Yeah, they were pretty scratched up," Max agreed. "We just threw them into the woods!"

"If they were that bad you should have put them in the trash," Kristy informed.

"We'll get them next time," Owen assured her.

When they finished their drinks Kari said, "I guess we will see you all at the airport next Saturday."

"Yes," Kristy affirmed, "see you then. And thanks for all your help!"

The kids ran out ahead of them and waited at the car.

"She thought they were garden Gnomes!" Max said in disbelief.

"Did you see the way they froze?" Owen asked.

"It was crazy!" Camden said.

"So, Gnomes are real?" asked Reaghan.

"It looks like they are," chuckled Brody.

"I love this house!" Max blurted out. Everyone laughed.

Kari came to the car, and they waved goodbye as she drove out of the driveway.

"Should I inspect the yard?" Kristy asked, as they watched them drive away.

"Sure! We cleaned it all up." Owen said as they walked towards the back.

When they came around the corner, Kristy stopped, and looking at the bush they had found Lilly in she asked, "What happened here?" Owen hadn't really looked at the bush after they got Lilly out of it. They had chopped almost half of it away trying to free her.

"We trimmed it!" Max said, oblivious to how bad it looked.

Kristy shook her head, "Maybe we will leave the trimming to your father next time," and they all laughed.

Monday morning as the boys got ready for school Owen said, "I'm a little worried about taking the stones to school."

"We all agreed that it would be ok!" Max assured him.

"You worry too much!" Brody chimed in, "It will be fine!"

"I hope so," Owen answered.

They went downstairs for breakfast and then got in the car. When they got to the drop-off line Mom said, "Have a good day! Love you!"

"Love you too Mom!" they said and got out of the car.

Mr. Swingler was there greeting everyone again. "Good to see you this morning boys!" he said with a smile.

"Is he out here every day?" Max wondered out loud, as they walked past. Mr. Swingler overheard him and answered, "Yes! I am!" Max laughed, looking back, and Mr. Swingler winked at him.

At recess Max and Brody saw Camden and went running over to him. "I didn't know we had the same recess," Max said.

"Technically we aren't supposed to, but the school is working on the other playground so now we are sharing this one," Camden informed. He and two of his friends were throwing a football around. "These are my friends, Noah and Cameron," he introduced. Then told his friends, "These are my two cousins that just moved to town last summer, Max and Brody."

"Hi," they both said to the twins.

Just then another boy came running up to them and said, "Hey Camden, are these your cousins that moved to town?"

"Yes," he answered. "Jaxon, this is Max and Brody."

Max and Brody both said, "Hi!"

"Let's go play Mega 4 Squares!" Brody suggested, and they all got in the line of kids waiting to play.

When Max got in the game Camden whispered to Brody, "Do you think he can resist using his powers?"

"He can," Brody answered confidently.

There was no sign that Max had used his powers as he played. He moved into the Kings position, and Brody and Camden were both in the game. None of the children slipped and used their powers.

Owen was also controlling his mind reading power. When he had a quiz in English he never once tried to get the answer from anyone's head.

While he was in homeroom with Mrs. Rinella, she asked him about his twin brothers. "I can't remember what their names are!" she joked. "Maybe I'll just call them Mac and Wac!" The whole class laughed at that.

When the last bell rang, the kids all met outside the building, waiting for their ride home.

"How did it go with the stones?" Owen asked.

"Good!" Camden said, "How about the rest of you?"

"There were no problems!" Max informed.

"It was fine!" Reaghan agreed. "Even during gym today, I didn't let my ninja powers out!"

Kristy pulled up and Owen, Max, and Brody hopped in the car, and Kari was right behind her.

CHAPTER 4
The Homecoming

Saturday had come quickly, and the boys were excited to get to the airport. They had made a giant sign that said, 'Welcome Home, Dad!!'. Kari, Camden, and Reaghan were there also, and they waited anxiously as the passengers came through the tunnel, exiting the plane.

"There they are!" shouted Brody as he spotted them. A minute later Adam and Austin emerged from the tunnel and the kids ran to them, throwing their arms around their necks.

"Who are these grown boys?" Adam asked, winking at Kristy. "What did you do with our kids?"

The boys all laughed and said, "It's us, Dad!"

Austin scooped up Reaghan and gave her a big hug, then held out his hand to Camden saying, "And who is this young man?"

"Dad!" Reaghan scolded, "that's Camden!"

"It can't be!" Austin teased, then gave him a big hug also.

Everyone talked at the same time as they made their way to the baggage claim. "Slow down!" Adam said. "We'll be home for two weeks, so you don't have to ask everything right now!"

"Only two weeks?" Kari and Kristy said simultaneously.

"As we were leaving, we got new orders," Austin apologized. "I would have let you know sooner but..."

"This one shouldn't be as long away though," Adam explained. "Maybe just a month."

"We should be back before Thanksgiving!" said Austin.

"And then be home at least through December!" Adam added.

"Well, we will just have to pack in as much fun as we can," Kristy sighed.

"Wait till you see our house!" Owen said excitedly, "There are so many trees for the zipline!"

Adam looked at Austin, "I'll barbecue if you come over to help?"

Austin laughed, "I think I can do that!"

"We can plan something for next weekend," Kristy suggested.

"Sounds good," Kari agreed, "let me know what I can bring."

They exited the airport chatting about all the things they could do and then separated, each family heading home.

As Kristy and Adam drove into the driveway Adam whistled, "That is one big house!"

"It's a really cool house too!" Owen added.

"Yeah, we love living here!" Max shouted. Brody nodded in agreement.

Adam laughed, "Well, let's go in and check out this really cool house."

They got out of the car and the boys started running to the door. Adam ran with them, enjoying their excitement.

"Close your eyes!" Owen instructed, so Adam put his hand over his eyes. Brody opened the door and Max and Owen led him into the entryway.

"You can open them!" Brody shouted.

Adam took his first look at the large house, "Wow, this really is cool," he said, giving Kristy a glance. The boys took him through the whole house, showing him all the rooms, and then took him outside into the backyard.

"Look at all the woods, Dad!" Max said, "We could put up a bunch of ziplines!"

"We could," Adam agreed, "except the trees are pretty thick, we will need to thin them out a little."

"Follow me!" Owen instructed, "I'll show you where we want it."

Adam followed all the boys a short distance into the woods where they stopped at one of the larger trees.

"We could put the start of it here," said Owen. "There's plenty of room to build a platform, and then we could end it over there."

"That just might work," Adam observed. "Good job boys! Later this week we can go shopping for everything we'll need. How much exploring have you done in these woods?"

"A lot!" answered Max.

Adam laughed, "I have no doubt! You'll have to show me what you found."

"There is a nice creek not too far from here," Brody said, "and I saw some fish in it."

"Did you catch anything?" asked Adam.

"We haven't actually fished in it yet," Brody confessed.

"Why not?" Adam questioned.

The boys all looked at each other, "We've been busy doing other things," Owen explained.

"Let's go back to the house," Adam suggested, "and see what your Mom is up to."

They walked back to the house laughing and chatting about the woods and the zipline. Kristy had made dinner in the crockpot and Adam announced, "That smells really good! When do we eat?"

"As soon as all of you get washed up!" she told them, smiling.

The boys ran upstairs. Adam wrapped his arms around Kristy, "It's so good to be home."

As the boys washed their hands they whispered to each other, "I wish we could tell Dad all about the stones and Jack," Max confessed.

"And Lilly," Brody added.

"Me too," agreed Owen, "but I feel like it's not the right time."

When the boys came running back into the kitchen, they saw their parents kissing. "Gross, Dad!" Max hooted.

"Someday you won't think kissing girls is gross," Adam teased.

While they sat at the table eating, Adam asked, "So how is school going?"

"Good," they all said simultaneously.

Kristy looked at Adam, "That's what I get too. Your questions must be more specific."

"Ok," Adam said, trying again. "Owen, did you go out for the baseball team?"

"Yes," he replied.

Adam waited a minute, "Did you make it?"

"Yes," Owen said. "The first game is this Thursday, so you can come!"

"Wild horses couldn't keep me away!" Adam answered.

Max looked at him, "Huh?"

Adam and Kristy laughed. She explained, "That means he wouldn't miss it for anything."

"Oh," Max said, then kept eating.

"How about you Brody, do you like your teacher?" Adam questioned.

"Yes," he answered.

Adam looked at Kristy, and she chuckled.

Adam thought about it for a minute, then asked again, "Who are your new friends?"

This time Brody had more information as he named off several new boys he had met. Max added to the list of names also. "Maybe we can invite them over when you finish the zipline!" Max added, and Brody agreed.

"I'm sure we can," Kristy said. "We should have all your new friends over to visit while your Dad is home."

The boys were excited about that and started talking about everything they wanted to show them.

"Did you know they all thought our house was haunted?" Max asked Adam.

Adam looked surprised and asked, "Why?"

The boys were quiet for a second, not sure what to say, when Kristy spoke up, "There is an old legend about a black, hairy thing that lives in these woods."

"Oh, that sounds interesting!" Adam said. "Have you been looking for it, Owen?"

Owen shrugged, "Not really, it's just an old tale." Max kicked him under the table and Owen frowned at him.

"I'm sure there are a lot of animals living in these woods," Adam confirmed.

"There are!" Brody pipped up.

"What have you seen?" Adam asked.

"Uuh...," Brody stammered, looking for help from his brothers.

"I saw deer," Owen interrupted.

"I saw a fox!" Brody said.

"I saw a little creature by the trees!" Max blurted excitedly. This time Owen kicked Max under the table. Frowning at Owen, Max added, "It was probably a chipmunk or squirrel."

On Sunday morning, as they were getting ready for church, Owen asked, "Dad, do you go to church when you're on assignment?"

Adam smiled at him, "There isn't a church building that I can go to most of the time, but I'm always talking to God. I know He is always with me, and that gives my soul peace when I go into a dangerous situation."

"Do you ever get afraid?" Brody asked.

"Yes," Adam answered. "But even in that fear I know God is with me."

"Can you tell us about one of those times?" Owen asked.

Adam pondered the question, "I'll think about that, perhaps there is one I can tell you about."

Kristy gave him a concerned look. "It will be PG," he assured her.

When they got to the church Kari and Austin were already there, so they went into the sanctuary together. After the worship songs the children were dismissed for Childrens' Church, which was in the basement.

When the service was over, they met up with the children in the hallway. "Does anyone want to go out for lunch?" Kari suggested.

"Chinese!" shouted Reaghan.

"Yeah, Chinese!" Brody seconded.

Everyone agreed, so they headed to the China Buffet. During lunch Adam asked Austin, "When can you come over and help me set up this zipline?"

Austin looked at Kari and laughing asked, "What do you have planned for me this week?"

"I want to get those basement stairs finished while you are home," she answered, "but that's all I have on your to-do list."

"I still have to get all the supplies, so maybe not till next weekend?" Adam suggested.

"Yeah!" Owen added. "That way we can help!"

"Saturday morning it is!" Austin confirmed.

Chapter 5
The Race

Monday morning on the way to school, Max was telling Adam about a boy named Joshua that he beat in a race the first week of school. "I don't think he likes me," Max said. "He is always trying to one-up me."

"How?" Adam asked.

"Well, at recess if we play basketball, he is always fouling me, and then argues that it was not a foul," Max explained. "Last week he just came up behind me and shoved me down."

"What did you do?" questioned Adam.

"I got up and told him to knock it off," answered Max, "and there was a teacher out there that saw him do it, so he had to go sit on the bench."

"You handled that well," Adam told him. "Maybe just don't play with him at recess."

"I don't try to, but it's just a pick-up game so anyone can join," explained Max.

"I don't want you to ever start a fight, but don't be afraid to stand up for yourself," Adam told him as they pulled up to the school.

Mr. Swingler was there to open the car door as usual. "You must be Mr. Daniels," he said to Adam, reaching in to shake his hand.

"Yes sir," Adam replied, "nice to meet you Mr. Swingler. The kids told me you would be here at the sidewalk."

Mr. Swingler laughed, "Everyday!"

The boys jumped out of the car, waving goodbye, and walked into the building. Joshua was also walking into the building and purposely bumped into Max as he hurried past.

"What is your problem?!" Max hollered at him, but he just kept going.

"Just ignore him," Brody suggested.

"It's hard to ignore someone as they push you around," Max growled as they walked into their classroom. He hung up his backpack and went to his seat. Joshua sat right across from him and mumbled something that Max did not understand.

"Do you have something to say to me?" Max asked, glaring at him.

"I've always been the best athlete in this class, and don't you forget it!" Joshua snarled.

Max continued to stare at him, "You're mad because I beat you fair and square in a foot race?"

"I want a re-match!" Joshua announced. "You won't beat me again!"

"Fine!" agreed Max, "When and where?"

"After school tomorrow, on the junior high track," Joshua stated. "We will race one lap around."

"I'll be there," Max confirmed. "And if I win, you back off and stop harassing me."

Joshua stared at him, "Agreed, but you will not win."

The rest of that day Joshua would snicker at Max any time they passed each other, but he didn't push him, or bump into him.

After school Max was telling Owen about what happened and about the race.

"Max, you better not wear your stone tomorrow for that race," Owen warned, "I think you would be too tempted to use its power just to prove him wrong."

"I was thinking the same thing," Brody agreed.

"I'd really like to use it, just to teach him a lesson," Max confessed, "but I'll take it off before the race."

The next day Max was a little nervous. He really wanted to beat Joshua but wondered if that would just make him more of a bully.

After the last bell, Max discreetly took his stone pouch off and placed it under some of his papers in his desk. Then he and Brody headed out to the junior high track. Max was surprised to see a crowd of kids there.

"I thought it was just going to be the two of us," he confessed nervously to Brody.

"Joshua must want everyone to see him beat you," Brody said.

Max just looked at him. "Not that he is going to!" Brody clarified. "You can beat him easily!"

Just then Owen came running up to them, "Did you take your stone off?" he whispered.

Max nodded yes.

They got to the track and the kids started clapping. Then Joshua stepped up, "Quiet down!" he yelled at everyone. "This race is to settle which one of us is the fastest, and that's always been me!" Some of the kids cheered him, while others booed. He waved his hands in the air, and everyone grew quiet. "You ready, Daniels?"

Max nodded and stepped up to the start line.

Brody said, "I'll give you the start signal," and started to walk to the front of them.

"Not you!" Joshua complained, "You probably have some sort of secret signal to give him a head start."

Brody asked, "Who do you want then?"

One of the girls in the crowd, Hanley, stepped up and said, "I can do it."

Joshua studied her for a second, then said, "Ok."

Hanley stood about 5 feet in front of them and raised her hand. "Ready," she hollered.

Both Max and Joshua looked straight ahead.

"Set," she hollered again.

The boys set their feet.

"Go! Hanley yelled.

Max leapt across the start line, focused on the track ahead, pumping his arms and legs as fast as he could. Joshua was right beside him, keeping pace. They were neck and neck going into the first turn, then Max dropped behind him, keeping pace, step for step. As they came out of the turn Max moved over to his side again. Joshua glanced over at him with a worried look. He thought he would be way ahead of Max by now. As they got closer to the finish Max turned on as much speed as he could and started to pull ahead. He could hear the kids all cheering, and he glanced over at Joshua, who was only a few inches behind him. They both ran as fast as they could towards the finish line. As they crossed the line Max wasn't sure if he had won. Joshua had stayed right by his side. The crowd of kids gathered around both boys as they collapsed onto the grass, gasping for air.

"That was awesome!" one boy yelled. "You two were flying across that track!"

"You two are faster than the high school kids!" another boy hollered.

"Who won?" gasped Joshua.

"Who cares!" said an unfamiliar voice. The kids all parted and let a young teacher move through them to the boys still lying on the grass. "Boys," he said, "I'm the new high school track coach, and that was one of the best races I've seen! What grade are you in?"

Max and Joshua looked at each other. "Fourth," they said in unison.

"Wow!" The coach continued. "When you are freshmen, you better come see me! We could go to state with you two working together!" The coach walked away, still shaking his head in disbelief.

Joshua got up, looked at Max, and held his hand out to help him up. Max studied his face for a second, then took his hand.

"Truce?" Max asked.

Joshua slapped him on the back, maybe a little harder than he needed to, and said, "I guess we are better working together, than against each other." Then he walked away, talking with his friends.

Max, Brody, and Owen watched him go. "That worked out better than I had expected," Brody confessed.

"I thought I could beat him," Max admitted. "He is fast."

"I think you had him by an inch," Owen said, smiling, and they walked back to the school.

They all went back into the building to Max's classroom. He went to his desk and opened it, shuffling some papers around.

"Oh no!" Max whispered. "It's gone!"

"What?" said Owen. "Are you sure that's where you put it?"

"Yes!" Max half shouted. "I put it right here!"

The boys all went to the desk and emptied everything out of it. There was no stone pouch.

"Who would have taken it?" Owen asked.

"There was no one here when I put it in there!" insisted Max. "Nobody could have seen me!"

"Is there someone that stays after class?" Owen asked. "Maybe they go through the desks for the teacher?"

"No, not that I know of," Max answered.

Owen took his stone out of its pouch. "This is bad," he said. "Brody, is your stone working?"

Brody took his stone out, "It's not glowing." Then he looked around the room, "My eyesight is normal again. What are we going to do?"

"Right now, we have to go home," Owen informed. "Dad's waiting for us out in the parking lot."

They slowly walked out of the school, worried about how they could find who took the stone.

That evening, after dinner, the boys went upstairs to Owens bedroom. As they discussed what they were going to do, Owen's iPad started ringing. "It's Camden," Owen said, as he answered it. "Hello".

"Owen!" Camden sounded frantic. "Something's wrong with the stones!"

"We know," Owen answered. Then, making sure his bedroom door was closed, he told Camden what had happened at school that day.

"What are we going to do?" Camden asked.

"We were just discussing that," Owen told him.

"I could let the teacher know that someone took it from my desk," Max suggested.

"The rest of us could ask around, see if anyone heard someone talking about taking it," Camden added.

"I don't know what else to do," Owen said, "Let's hope this works."

Brody looked at Owen, "We could really use your mind reading powers now."

"For sure," Owen responded. "We could find the thief right away."

The next morning Max told his teacher that he was missing a pouch with a clear stone in it. "Could you maybe ask the class if anyone has found it?" he asked.

When the bell rang the teacher said, "Class, Max is missing a small pouch with a clear stone in it. Does anyone remember seeing it?"

The kids shook their heads no.

"Can you keep an eye out for it?" she asked, then looking at Max said, "I'm sure if anyone sees it, they will let you know, Max."

Max tried to catch the eye of the students, hoping someone would look guilty, but no one did. His mind was only half listening to the lesson as worried about how he could find his stone. When recess came, he and Brody met up with Camden and Reaghan.

"Any luck?" Camden asked.

"No," Max said sadly. "I don't know how I will ever find it."

"There has to be a way," Reaghan encouraged.

"We can strategize tonight," Camden offered, "My Dad is coming over to help clear away some trees for the zipline, so we are all coming for dinner."

The day dragged on for Max, who couldn't concentrate on school. The last bell finally rang, and he and Brody went out to wait for their Dad.

"Hi boys!" greeted Adam. "How was school?"

"Good," they answered, unenthusiastically.

Adam laughed, "Well, I know what will get you excited. Austin is coming over tonight to help me get the zipline up."

"Yeah, Camden told us," Brody informed.

"I thought you'd be more excited," Adam observed.

"We are, Dad," Owen assured.

"I'll take your word for it, because your faces don't show it," Adam chuckled. "You will all need to lend a hand while we clear out some trees and bushes."

"We will," they all agreed.

Shortly after they got home Austin and Kari drove in with the kids.

"Who's ready to work?" Austin shouted, faking enthusiasm. He pulled out a chain saw from the back of his truck as Adam came out of the house.

"I'll show you my plan," Adam told Austin, as they walked to the back yard. While they discussed what needed to be cleared, the kids huddled by the woods edge, discussing what happened at school.

Owen said, "I asked my friends if they heard anyone talking about your stone, but no one had."

"Finding a clear stone in a pouch probably wouldn't stir up too much excitement," Camden informed.

"You mean stealing," Max corrected.

The Dads had started clearing a path through the woods, so the kids moved farther away from the noise. They had moved into the woods, and Reaghan motioned to a tree a few yards away. "It's Lilly!" she whispered.

The boys looked at the Dads, but they were too busy to notice the small creature by the tree. Reaghan went over to her. "I wonder if she knows that we lost one of the stones," she asked the boys as she bent down. Lilly came to her but did not crawl into her lap as she had before. This time Lilly looked intently into Reaghan's eyes, "I wish I could tell her what happened."

All the boys knelt down, wondering if they could let her know, somehow, that a stone was lost. Lilly seemed to examine each boy's face and when she came to Max, she paused. Then she went to him and climbed onto his knee. She reached up to touch his face for a second, then got down and hurried back to her tree hallow.

"Do you think she knows?" Brody asked.

"It sure seemed like it," Owen observed.

"If we could take her to school, maybe she would know who took it?" Max wondered.

"We can't just shove her into a backpack," Owen scolded.

"But we could possibly bring the school to her!" Brody said, excitedly.

"Huh?" Reaghan questioned.

"The zipline!" Brody went on. "We could bring the class out here!"

"But I don't think she is going to go up to each kid and touch their face!" Max pointed out.

"Maybe she wouldn't have to, maybe she could tell from a distance," Reaghan suggested.

"It's worth a try," Camden said.

"Agreed," piped Owen. "Let's get busy helping so they can get it up!"

The kids worked all evening hauling branches to a burn pile. By the time they had the path cleared, it was getting too dark to continue. "We'll have to quit for tonight," Adam announced. "Maybe we can get it strung tomorrow, if Uncle Austin is available?"

"Please, Dad!" begged Camden and Reaghan.

Austin laughed, "I suppose, if Aunt Kristy wants to feed us supper again."

"I suppose I can," Kristy laughed.

"I can come in the morning if you want to get it finished tomorrow," Austin told Adam.

"Yes!" the kids chimed. "We want to have the class over this weekend! Can I invite them over Mom?" Max begged.

Kristy looked at Adam, "Will it be ready?"

"I think we can handle that," he answered, slapping Austin on the shoulder.

"Ok," Kristy said to Max, "I will send a note with you tomorrow and your teacher can tell the class."

"Thanks Mom!" Max whooped.

The next day Max and Brody handed their teacher the note and she read it to the class. "Mrs. Goodson's 4th grade class is invited to try the new zipline at Max and Brody's house this Saturday morning. We will start at 10:00 A.M. and then have a hotdog roast for lunch. Please come and bring your parents so we can get to know all of you." Chatter arose from the class. "Quiet class," Mrs. Goodson chided, "Mrs. Daniels sent an invitation for each of you to take home to your parents."

The kids couldn't wait to get home that evening to see how far their Dads had gotten with the zipline. Kari was there to pick them all up. "Is it done?" Camden asked.

"I don't know," Kari answered, "I haven't been over there yet today."

When they got to the house the kids piled out of the car and ran to the backyard.

"Wow!" said Reaghan. They all stared at the new platform built up around the first tree, with the zipline careening down the wooded slope to another platform where it ended.

"Dad, this looks awesome!" Owen shouted at Adam who was standing on the second platform.

Both Adam and Austin were installing the brake system on the line. They waived at the kids, then went back to work.

Kari walked up to them saying, "It looks nearly done! Why don't we go in the house and grab a snack while they finish up?"

As they walked back to the house Owen declared, "I get first try!"

"I get second!" Camden shouted.

"It should be youngest first!" Reaghan suggested, but no one agreed to that.

Brody said, "Owen, you can go first, that way if it doesn't work you will be the one that crashes."

"Yeah!" agreed Max, laughing.

As the kids finished their snack, Adam and Austin came in the house.

"I think it's ready to test," Adam announced.

"I'll go first!" volunteered Owen.

"Austin and I are going to test it first," Adam informed.

"We wouldn't want you kids to get hurt," Austin said.

"I think you two just want to have the first ride," chided Kari.

The men looked at each other innocently, "What?" Austin objected, "It's always safety first!"

"Yeah, right!" Kristy laughed. "But I agree, you need to try it out first," then she added with a wink, "if it will hold you."

Both men sucked in their guts in protest. "It's approved for 380 pounds," Adam informed. "Let's give it a try!"

The kids ran out the door, excitedly, followed by the adults.

Adam demonstrated how the harness went and explained how the brake worked. Then he climbed up the platform and hooked onto the line. Austin went up with him and held the seat as Adam got on. He nodded at Austin to let it go and careened down the hill. The kids all cheered. When he got to the end of the line the large spring break quickly slowed him down and he glided easily onto the second platform. He gave a thumbs-up to the group as he slipped out of the harness. Austin pulled the seat back to the first platform with the rope and said, "Who wants to go first?"

"I do!" hollered Owen, as he climbed up the platform.

Austin helped him get into the harness, "Ready?"

Owen nodded. Austin gave him a push and he was on his way.

Adam was at the second platform waiting for him. Owen was all smiles when he reached it.

"That was so fun!" he beamed.

"I'm next!" said Camden, as he climbed up to Austin. Everybody took a turn and then went again.

When Reaghan was getting buckled into the harness, she noticed a small movement in the crook of the tree. As she stared at the spot, Lilly's head suddenly appeared, just for a second, then was gone. When she finished her ride, she walked back to the group and whispered, "I saw Lilly in the tree, just for a second. There must be a hollow up there."

"Which tree?" asked Max.

"The first one, where we get on," she answered.

"That's great!" whispered Brody. "Maybe she will be able to tell if someone has the stone!"

Owen had just gotten off the line and came walking over. "What are you whispering about?" he asked.

"I saw Lilly," Reaghan informed. "There has to be a hollow up there."

Owen looked up at the tree. "Maybe that will help her know who has the stone."

"That's what I said," Brody told him.

"This just might work!" Camden said, excitedly.

CHAPTER 6
The Zipline

By Friday, all the kids had returned the permission slip that Kristy had sent home with them saying they could come on Saturday. Max had high hopes that Lilly would, somehow, be able to tell who had taken his stone.

Saturday morning all the boys were up early. Kristy was having a cup of coffee in the kitchen when they walked downstairs.

"You are up early!" Kristy greeted.

"I'm too excited to sleep!" Max confessed.

"What time is everyone coming?" Brody asked.

"Not until 10:00 o'clock," she answered. "What do you want for breakfast?"

"Can we get donuts?" Owen asked.

"When your Dad gets up, I'll send him to the store," Kristy agreed.

The boys grabbed their iPads and went back upstairs into Owens room. Max couldn't concentrate on the game he was playing. "What am I going to do if this doesn't work?" he worried.

"It's going to work," Owen assured. "It has to."

The morning dragged on. Camden, Reaghan, Aunt Kari, and Uncle Austin showed up about 9:00.

"There are some donuts left if you want one," Kristy told them.

Camden and Reaghan each took one and all the kids went out the back door.

"I've never seen them so worried about something before," Kristy said.

"I know!" Kari agreed. "They were up super early, wanting to come over." She looked out the window. The kids were at the edge of the woods in a small huddle. "I wonder what they are plotting."

The kids walked to the edge of the woods, by the tree where Lilly had disappeared.

"Lilly," Reaghan called softly. To her amazement, she appeared from the hollow. "If you can understand me," Reaghan went on, "we need your help today. There will be a lot of kids here pretty soon, and we need you to tell us if one of them has Max's stone."

Lilly stood at the base of the tree, cocking her head, like she was trying to understand. Then she quickly disappeared back into the tree hollow.

"I hope she understood," Camden said.

The kids started arriving and Kristy and Adam greeted them and their parents. Kari and Austin already knew many of them and showed them to the backyard, where there were tables and chairs set up. Once everyone was there, Adam and Austin positioned themselves at each end of the zipline. The kids excitedly lined up for their turn.

As each child took their turn Owen and the others watched the trees for any sign of Lilly. The classmates were on their second turn before they saw her, briefly, when a boy named Parker was getting hooked up.

"Did you see that?" Brody whispered.

"Yes," Owen answered. "He must have it."

"But how do we get it from him?" Max questioned.

"We'll have to get him away from everyone to confront him," Camden said.

"Maybe we can lure him into the woods," Owen suggested. "What do you know about him?" he asked Max.

"I don't think I ever talked to him," Max confessed. "He doesn't ever say anything in class."

When Parker got off the zipline Max walked over to him, "Did you like it?" Max asked, trying to start a conversation.

"Yeah, it's a lot of fun!" Parker answered.

"Do you like the woods?" Max asked again.

"I guess," Parker shrugged. "I haven't been in them very much."

"These woods are really cool," Max went on. "Maybe I can show you some of it later."

"Maybe," Parker said, then got back in the line.

Max walked over to Owen, "Maybe after the hotdog roast, I can get him to come with me into the woods. He didn't seem too excited about it though."

"Tell him about the fallen tree over the creek," Owen suggested. "Maybe you can get him to come with you to see it."

Owen motioned for Max, Brody, Camden, and Reaghan to follow him and when they were away from the crowd told them his plan. "After lunch Max is going to bring Parker into the woods to see the fallen tree by the creek. The rest of us need to be there waiting for them. Then we can confront him about the stone."

Kari and Kristy were getting the things from the house for lunch. Once they had everything ready Kristy announced, "You can take one last ride, then come to the table and we will start roasting hot dogs!"

Reaghan noticed Lilly by the base of the tree again. She would pop out for a second, then go back in.

"I think Lilly is trying to tell us something," she told Max. They walked over to the tree to see if she would come out again. As they waited Max noticed some of the other Gnomes peeking out from other trees in the woods.

"Look!" he whispered to Reaghan. "There are a bunch of them here."

"Something must be wrong," Reaghan whispered back.

"I'll go get the others," Max informed, and walked back over to the crowd of kids by the table. He tapped Owen on the shoulder, nodding for him to follow. They went to the others and did the same, then walked back over to Reaghan.

"What's up?" Owen asked.

"Look," Reaghan said, and nodded into the woods.

As they looked Brody said, "Wow! Why are they all here?"

Camden followed his gaze and gasped a little as he saw little Gnome heads in nearly every tree.

"What the heck?" Max whispered. "What do you think they want?"

"I don't know," Owen answered. "I need my power to understand them."

As they watched, the little heads started to move from tree to tree. They were moving down the edge of the woods, toward the road.

The kids just stood there and watched until Lilly popped out of the tree next to Owen and pulled on his pants leg.

"Gosh!" Owen said, startled. "She scared me to death!"

Lilly was already back in the tree when the others looked at him.

"Huh?" Brody said.

"Lilly," Owen explained, "she just pulled on my pant leg!"

As the kids looked, Lilly appeared again. She ran to Camdens leg and tugged on him this time, then ran back to the tree.

"Is she trying to tell us something?" Camden questioned.

As they watched the tree, Lilly appeared again, this time running towards the other Gnomes. She stopped for a second, looking at the kids, then made a motion with her hand that said follow me, and disappeared into a tree.

The kids looked back at the bonfire. No one was paying attention to them, they were all getting hot dogs on sticks, ready to roast them.

"Come on," Owen whispered, and they slipped out of sight down the side of the house.

"Do you see them?" Camden asked. Everyone scoured the woods looking for any sign of motion.

"There!" Max said, pointing to the trees in the front yard.

The kids hurried to the front, looking for Lilly and her friends. "Look!" shouted Reaghan, "over by the fountain!" Some of the Gnomes were darting in and out of small holes in the ground at its base.

Owen and the others walked over, when suddenly, one of the Gnomes climbed up Owen's clothing and sat on his shoulder. He froze, not knowing if it was trying to hurt him, or talk to him. As Camden watched, one of them climbed up his clothing as well and sat on his shoulder.

"What should we do?" Camden whispered to the others, afraid to move.

Then Lilly came out and climbed up Reaghan's clothes while another one climbed up Brody. Lilly started to reach into Reaghan's shirt neck, feeling for the string that held the stone around her neck.

"What is it, Lilly?" Reaghan asked.

"She is trying to steal my stone!" Brody cried, as the Gnome on his shoulder did the same thing.

"Wait," Owen urged everyone, "Let's see what they want." He lifted his stone pouch up over his head and showed it to the Gnome on his shoulder. The little creature pulled the stone out of the pouch and laid it in his hand, its eyes studying his face.

Reaghan took her stone out of its pouch and held it out to Lilly, "Do you want to see it?" she asked her. Lilly pushed the stone back to Reaghan, then looked at Camden.

"Camden," Reaghan instructed, "take the stone out of the pouch and hold it."

Once all the kids had their stones in their hands the Gnomes quickly climbed down and scurried over to the fountain. They seemed very excited, jumping up and down.

"I don't know what you are trying to tell me," Owen said as he sat on the edge of the fountain looking at his stone.

Max walked over, studying the fountain that stood in his front yard. He had never really paid attention to it, but now he examined it. It was round, with an angel standing in the middle of it, holding one hand up to the sky, with the other holding a jug at her waist where water would pour out back into the reservoir if it was working. As he studied it, he gasped a little. There were small hieroglyphics carved into her dress. "Aren't these the same markings that are on the chest we found the stones in?" he asked.

Everyone peered at the carvings in the angel's dress.

Lilly climbed back up to Reaghan's shoulder and excitedly chattered in her ear. "This must be what they were trying to show us," she said, "but why?"

Owen stepped into the fountain to move closer to the angel, feeling the few inches of cold water in the basin soaking into his shoes. Lilly suddenly leapt from Reaghan's shoulder to Owens and then leapt onto the angel's shoulder. "I don't know what it means, Lilly!" Owen told her, frustrated. She looked him straight in the eye and then climbed up the angel's arm, perching on top of her raised hand. Owen's gaze followed her when he suddenly realized what the angel held in her hand. "It's the stones!" he gasped. In the angel's hand were five small stones, each one resembling the stones they had found in the chest. Owen took his stone and held it up, like the fountain was doing. Disappointed, he stepped out of the fountain, "I thought maybe we were supposed to hold them up like that."

Lilly started to chatter again. "Owen, you stranded her in the fountain!" Reaghan scolded him.

"Oh, sorry Lilly!" Owen apologized, as he stepped back into the cold water of the fountain so she could hop back down on his shoulder, but she didn't come down.

"Lilly, this water is cold, come on!" Owen begged, but she continued to chatter, making a fuss. Suddenly, the other Gnomes were all visible, climbing onto the ledge of the fountain. They stood in a circle and held their hands up in the middle.

"What are they doing?" asked Brody.

Lilly made even more noise, bringing the kids' attention back to her. She kept tapping the stones in the statue's hand.

"That's it!" Brody shouted. "I think I know what she wants!"

Lilly jumped down onto Owens shoulder and he stepped out of the fountain.

"Everyone, come here!" Brody instructed. "Stand in a circle and hold your stones up. Max, you too!"

"But, I don't have my stone," Max said as he got in the circle.

"I know, but I think you need to be part of this," Brody told him.

Everyone took their stone in their fingers and held it up.

"What now?" asked Reaghan.

"Is something supposed to happen?" Camen added.

They lowered their hands, disappointed.

"I thought that would work," Brody confessed.

"Work how?" Camden questioned.

Brody shrugged.

Suddenly Lilly dashed to Owens hand, grabbing his stone, then jumped over to Reaghan, hanging on her arm.

"Hey!" Owen hollered.

Lilly climbed down to Reaghan's hand where she held her stone and grabbed it too.

"Grab her!" Owen shouted, but Lilly leapt to the ground with the two stones and dashed over to the edge of the fountain.

The kids all froze, afraid they would never get them back if she went underground.

As they watched, she gave one stone to another Gnome, and then the two of them held up the stones clicking them together. They did this a few times, then put the stones down and disappeared into the small hole.

"I thought those stones were gone!" Camden said, as Owen picked them up and gave one to Reaghan.

"I don't think she was stealing them," Reaghan said. "Did you see what they did?"

Just then Adam came around the side of the house, "What are you five doing over there? Come back and get your hot dog!"

"Coming, Dad!" yelled Owen. As Adam disappeared around the corner Owen said, "Everyone, quick! Get in the circle with your stones! This time we touch them together."

They formed the circle again with stones in hand, this time as they lifted them up, they clicked them together. When the stones touched, a bright light shot out of them, forcing everyone backwards like they had been pushed. All the kids were on the ground, stunned.

"What was that?!" Brody groaned.

"The stones are glowing!" Max noticed as he got up. "Do you have your powers back?"

Reaghan did some ninja flips as she got up saying, "Yup!"

Brody studied the fountain, seeing the hieroglyphics much clearer now.

"They are," Owen agreed. "We have to go back now, Mom is coming!"

CHAPTER 7
The Theif

Everyone hurried towards the house as Kristy came around the corner. "It's rude to leave your friends back here while you five go off on your own!"

"Sorry Mom!" Max said. "We are coming!"

They hurried back to the fire pit and joined the group that was roasting their hot dogs. Some of the kids had already finished and were putting marshmallows on their sticks for Smores.

"Owen," Camden whispered, "can you read Parker's mind to see if he has the stone?"

Owen concentrated for a second, then shook his head, "He's only thinking about his marshmallow right now. Max, you will need to bring up the stone to him, maybe then I can tell if he has it."

"I will," nodded Max, and he casually made his way over to Parker, poking his stick with the hot dog on it right next to Parkers marshmallow.

"Are you having fun?" Max asked, trying to start a conversation.

Parker looked at him, "Yes, thanks for inviting me."

"Sure!" Max answered him. Then there was an awkward silence. "We don't get to talk much in school," Max continued.

Parker nodded, "Our desks aren't close."

"Right," Max muttered. Another awkward pause. "Do you want to go into the woods with me after we eat? I can show you the tree bridge over the creek!"

"Um, yeah, sure," Parker agreed. "Who else is going?"

"Uh, well," Max stammered. "Anyone can come, if they want to." He was really hoping to get Parker alone so they could confront him.

Max walked back over to Owen, "I didn't know how to bring up the stone, so I asked him if he wanted to go into the woods to see the tree bridge."

"That might be better," Owen agreed. "We need to get him alone."

"Right," Max stammered, "but he thinks I'm taking everyone into the woods!"

"Why does he think that?" Owen questioned.

"Because I kind of told him anyone could go," Max confessed. Owen gave him a mad look. "I couldn't help it! He acted like he wouldn't go alone! I think he is afraid of the woods!"

"Ok," said Owen, "maybe we can get by with just a few others wanting to go."

Just then Joshua came over and said, "I hear you are taking a group into the woods to see some kind of tree bridge."

Max looked at Owen, "Um, yeah."

"We were going to take the kids that are done eating over there before Dad opens the zipline up again," Owen explained. "If you're still eating though you don't have to come!"

"I'm done!" Joshua said. "Let's go!"

"Max," Owen instructed. "Go see who else is going. I'll meet you over by the back deck with Josh."

Joshua corrected Owen, "It's Joshua."

"Oh, sorry," Owen said, rolling his eyes at Max, "Joshua."

Max tried to think who else to ask, then went to Camden, Reaghan, and Brody. "We are going to go into the woods with Parker and Joshua. Maybe if you three come I won't have to ask anyone else. Head over to the back deck and I'll get Parker." Max walked over to him saying, "There's a small group of us going now, why don't you come while we wait for the zipline to open again."

Parker looked over at the small group gathered by the deck at the edge of the woods, "Oh, ok," he agreed. Max placed his hand on Parker's shoulder to guide him over to the group, hoping no one would notice them leaving.

Once everyone got there, they quickly slipped into the woods, following the trail that led to the creek.

Parker asked nervously, "So, you never saw any strange, wild creatures in here?"

"No," lied Max. "Just the usual, deer and fox and such."

"Don't be such a scaredy-cat!" Joshua grumbled as he wandered off the path.

Max was irritated by Joshua's mean comment and added, "We have seen a few bears, so you need to stay close."

Joshua looked around and hurried back to the trail. Max grinned at Parker, who looked worried, and winked. Parker smiled, thinking Max was just kidding, but walked a little closer.

As Reaghan walked along, she noticed the Gnomes peeking out at various trees along the way. They were so good at blending in she was not worried that Parker or Joshua would notice.

When they came to the tree everyone stopped.

"This is it?" sneered Joshua.

Owen looked at him, "Go on across," he dared.

Joshua studied the tree but did not step on it. Reaghan pushed to the front and easily walked over to the other side.

Joshua was not going to be shown up by a little girl, so slowly stood up on the fallen tree. He inched his way across, having to stop once to catch his balance. Once on the other side he acted like it was no big deal and hollered over at Parker, "Come on, chicken!"

Parker glanced at Max with a worried look on his face.

"You can do it," Max whispered. "I'll walk right behind you."

Parker slowly stepped up onto the tree and inched his way across. He lost his balance a little and Max reached out to steady him. "Thanks," he whispered, and continued over the bridge.

Camden, Owen, and Brody crossed over behind them. Owen knew he had to bring up Max's stone to see if Parker had it, but he wasn't sure how to do it. He wanted to get him alone so suggested, "Joshua, you should go see the field that's down that trail. We usually see deer out there." Camden could see that Joshua was afraid to go, so said, "Come on, I'll go with you! There's nothing to be afraid of!"

"I'm not afraid!" Joshua stated. "I just don't know the way!"

"Right," Camden agreed, rolling his eyes at Owen, "I'll show you." They disappeared down the trail.

Parker did not seem to mind that no one asked him to go. He looked a little nervous.

Max looked at Owen, hoping he was in mind reading mode, then asked Parker, "Do you remember when I lost that stone in school, and the teacher asked if anyone had seen it?"

"Yes," Parker answered, "did you ever find it?"

Max looked at Owen, thinking Parker was a good liar, when Owen met his gaze. He was shaking his head, looking confused.

"It's not him," Owen said.

"What?" Parker asked.

"But Lilly..." Reaghan started.

"It's not him," Owen assured.

"What's not him?" Parker asked again.

"It's nothing," Max dismissed.

"Maybe we should go get Camden and Joshua," Owen suggested.

"I'd like to go back now," Parker said. "I want to ride the zipline again."

"Sure," Owen said, "Brody, do you want to take him back?"

"Ok," Brody agreed. "Come on Parker, I'll walk with you back over the tree."

Once they were over the tree and out of ear shot Max asked Owen, "Are you sure it wasn't him?"

"Yes!" Owen assured him. "He was truly sorry for you, that you hadn't found it."

"I don't get it!" Reaghan said. "I was sure Lilly pointed to him."

Just then Lilly popped out of a tree going down the trail that Camden and Joshua had gone down. She ran up to Owen, climbing up his pant leg to sit on his shoulder. Owen concentrated on her, trying to understand what she wanted. She looked him in the eye for a minute, then looked back down the path. Giving him one more look, she jumped down and ran to a tree, disappearing into it. Camden and Joshua came walking into the clearing.

Owen walked up to Joshua and stopped. "I think you have something that belongs to Max," he accused.

"I don't know what you're talking about!" Joshua blurted out.

Max realized what Lilly must have told Owen and walked up to Joshua, "You took my stone?"

"You're crazy!" Joshua complained and started to walk away. Max grabbed his shirt and saw the familiar string that was attached to the stone pouch. He grabbed it and pulled the pouch out of Joshua's shirt.

"What's this?" Max hollered.

Joshua tried to pull away, but Camden grabbed his arm. Joshua looked amazed at him as he tried to get free of his grip. Camden just smiled, and pulled the pouch over his neck, handing it to Max.

Max checked the stone inside, nodding at the others, "It's here," he confirmed.

The kids all surrounded Joshua while Camden kept hold. He looked terrified, stammering, "I found it! I didn't know it was yours!"

"What should we do with him?" Camden sneered.

"Look," Joshua begged, "You got it back!"

"No thanks to you!" Max growled.

"I'm sorry," Joshua continued, "I'll leave you alone! I won't bother you or your brother anymore!"

"Let him go Camden," Owen ordered. "He is not going to be a problem anymore."

Camden released his arm. Joshua rubbed the spot where Camden had held him, "You have some grip."

"Oh, that's nothing," Camden answered, "You should see when I really try."

"Let's go back to the house," Owen suggested. "We will just forget about this, right?" He stared at Joshua.

"Forget what?" Joshua responded.

The others laughed, "Exactly!" Camden agreed.

No one spoke as they walked back through the woods. When they hit the clearing Joshua ran back to the others. Max stopped and asked Owen, "Do you think he means it? Is he going to keep quiet and leave me alone?"

"Yes," Owen assured. "He is more worried that we will tell someone that he stole the stone in the first place."

Reaghan asked, "Did Lilly tell you he had the stone?"

"She did," smiled Owen.

"I wish I could understand her," mused Reaghan.

"I think you understand her pretty well," Owen told her. "She likes you the best."

Reaghan smiled big. She had thought her and Lilly had a special connection, even though she couldn't read her mind.

Brody came walking up to them, "How did it go?"

"Good," Max said, showing Brody the pouch now hanging around his neck.

"We better get back to the group," Brody prompted, "Mom's been asking where you were."

As they walked together Brody said, "Parker is pretty cool, once you get to know him. He told me no one had ever taken him into the woods before or let him ride a zipline."

When they got back to the group Kristy met them. "Where did you run off to?"

Owen answered her, "We took a couple of kids to see the tree bridge in the woods."

"Ok, but let's try to stay in the yard now," Kristy told him, looking slightly annoyed.

"We will, Mom," Owen assured her.

Adam and Austin were shutting down the zipline and the parents and kids were making their way to the front of the house, getting ready to leave. Parker walked over to Max and Brody saying, "Thanks for inviting me! I had a lot of fun. And thanks for taking me into the woods!"

"Maybe you can come over another time and play!" Suggested Brody. "There are a lot of neat things to see in the woods. We could go exploring!"

"I'd like that," Parker replied. Then he ran to his Mom's car and got in, waving goodbye.

Owen and Camden had been hanging back, watching the crowd leave, when they heard something back by the zipline. They turned to see what it was and gasped when they saw it. Joshua was up on the zipline by himself, trying to keep his balance at the top of the platform. He was partially hooked into the harness, but the seat was moving down the zipline, pulling him forward. He was desperately trying to unhook the harness so he wouldn't be pulled off the platform. Max, Brody, and Reaghan walked up, also seeing Joshua's problem.

"He's going to fall!" Brody warned.

That's when all their superpowers took over, it seemed, by instinct. Owen knew what the others were thinking, and directed them, "Max!" he hollered. "Get Camden underneath the platform!"

Reaghan had already started moving towards it in full ninja mode, quickly covering the distance between her and Joshua. She got there as he was still teetering on the edge, and quickly climbed her way to the top.

As she made her way, Max had grabbed Camden by the arm and, in super speed mode, pulled him to the platform. Reaghan reached the top and grabbed for Joshua, but he had already started falling. When Max released Camden, he was directly under Joshua. Camden was slightly disoriented from Max's speed, but looked up, just in time to catch the terrified boy. As Camden held him, Reaghan gracefully jumped down beside them. "Are you alright?" she gasped.

Joshua slowly opened his eyes. "What... How..." he stammered. Camden put him down.

"What were you thinking?" Max panted. "You could have been killed!"

"I just wanted to ride one more time," Joshua whimpered.

Owen and Brody came running up. "Are you trying to get yourself killed?" Brody hollered.

Joshua teared up, "I'm sorry! I thought I could do it by myself."

"You better go," Owen told him, "Your Mom is waiting for you."

Joshua looked at each one of them, then ran to the front of the house.

As the kids watched him go, they noticed both Adam and Austin standing at the corner of the house. They were both staring at the group of kids with their mouths open.

"Uh-oh," Camden said.

"Did they see all that?" Max asked.

Owen answered, "Yes, they did."

"Are they mad?" asked Reaghan.

"Not mad," Owen told her, "I'd say confused."

"What are we going to say?" Brody asked as they started walking towards them.

"Let's let them ask the questions," Owen suggested.

When they reached their Dads, they stopped without speaking. Kari and Kristy both called from the front yard, and the group walked in silence to them. The kids were sure they were in trouble and waited nervously for someone to speak.

"Your teacher is leaving; you should thank her for bringing the class out here." Kristy instructed.

Max and Brody walked up to her car, "Thank you Mrs. Goodson," they said in unison.

"Thank you for inviting all of us!" she answered. "See you Monday!"

When everyone had driven away Adam and Austin turned to the kids. "We need to have a family meeting. Everyone in the house," Adam ordered.

The kids all marched silently to the door, while the adults stood in the yard. They watched out the window as their parents discussed something.

"Can you read their minds?" asked Camden. "How much trouble are we in?"

"Mom told them about the diary already," Owen informed. "I think our Dads were surprised when they saw what our powers could do. They are coming in."

The adults turned and walked to the house. When they walked in the kids were all sitting at the dining room table. Everyone remained quiet for a minute. Then Kristy spoke up, "I showed everyone the diary I found in the attic, the one that talked about magic stones."

The kids sat very still.

"We know you wear them around your necks." Austin said.

"Let's see them," Adam ordered.

Each child slowly pulled their stone pouch from under their shirts, then dumped the stone out and set them on the table in front of them.

"We found them in a secret room in the basement," Owen confessed. "That extra set of keys the realtor brought over opened it."

"And it opened the chest that held the stones," Brody added.

"When we each picked up a stone, they started to glow," Max explained.

"All of a sudden I could see things on the wall that no one else could see," Brody informed.

"And I could 'see' them also," Owen added. "But not with my eyes. I was reading Brody's mind!"

"Each one of us had gotten a special power, all different from the others," Camden said.

"We saw some of those powers," Austin informed. "I'd say yours was strength?" he asked Camden. Then looked at Reaghan, "And yours is agility?" They both nodded.

Adam asked, "So if Owen got mind reading, and Brody got special eyesight, then I'm guessing from what I saw that Max got speed?"

"You should not have kept this from us," Kari scolded.

"We're sorry," Camden and Reaghan apologized.

"Once we figured out that we had powers, we realized quickly what they were for," Owen explained. "Mom, do you remember those hunters we met in the store?"

"Yes," she answered. "But they never came into the woods." She looked at Owens expression, "Did they?"

Owen went on, "Do you remember the tale of the big, black, hairy thing that lives in these woods?"

"Yes," she answered.

"Well, it was real," Owen said. "We met it, and I could read it's mind."

"I'm confused," Adam interrupted.

"There is a rumor about this house and the woods behind it," Kristy informed.

"I've heard the rumor," Kari confessed, "but never thought it was real!"

"Jack needed our help because those hunters were trying to kill him and his family!" Reaghan interjected.

"I found their secret cave opening," Brody added. "It is under that old deck in the back."

"Wait, wait!" Austin hollered. "Who is Jack?"

"He was the young sasquatch that followed us in the woods," Reaghan said matter-of-factly.

"He followed us a few times, and the stones helped me communicate with him," Owen tried to explain.

"We had to set a trap for the hunters, to scare them out of the woods!" Max said.

"Is that the day you asked me to let you go into the woods?" Kristy asked. "When you were grounded?"

"It is," Owen admitted, "I didn't have time to explain then, but Jack's father sent me a message that the hunters were coming."

"We only had a few minutes until they would be in the area where we had set the trap," Camden added. "We barely got there in time."

"But it worked!" Max said, excitedly. "We each got to our stations and scared them half to death!"

"They ran out of the woods like scared kids!" Brody laughed. When he realized the adults were not laughing, he stopped.

The four adults stared at each other. After a minute Adam looked at Kristy, "What kind of house did your Aunt Barbie leave us?'

"A great house!" Max answered.

Adam started to laugh.

"I'm not sure this is funny!" Kari scolded. "Someone could have gotten hurt!"

"I think these stones are a pretty good insurance policy that they will not get hurt," Austin said. "Let me show you. Kids, let's go outside."

They all got up and headed out the back door.

"Let's see what you got," Austin instructed.

The kids looked confused, but Owen knew what he meant. "Max, how fast can you run around the house?" he asked.

"Y-You mean," Max stammered.

"Yes," Owen said, "that's exactly what I mean."

Max smiled really big. He took off in super mode just as Kari started to say something and was back before she got the first word out.

Owen looked at the adults, then smiled. "Reaghan, how hard would it be for you to get up on the zipline platform?" he asked her. Without hesitation she bounded across the yard, flipping over any chair or table that was in her way, then with ninja-like agility climbed up to the platform without using the ladder. She paused for a second at the top, then leapt over to the nearest tree, using the branches like a gymnast on the way down. Then she skipped back to the group.

"Camden," Owen suggested, "maybe you could help clear away that big tree trunk that our Dads couldn't move."

"Watch this, Dad!" Camden hollered, as he ran over to the fallen tree.

"No way!" shouted Austin in disbelief as Camden bent down and grabbed the tree.

Camden laughed, then picked up the end of the tree. He looked at the length of it, then dropped it.

"Don't hurt yourself!" hollered Kari.

Camden walked to the middle of the tree, looked back at the group, then picked it up, this time lifting the whole thing off the ground. "Where do you want it?" he asked.

Adam looked at Austin in shock, then hollered back, "put it on the burn pile!"

Camden walked it over to the pile of burnt branches, then slammed one end of the tree down on the ground, breaking it in half. "It will fit better now!" He informed Adam.

As Camden walked back to the group, Owen looked over at Brody and asked, "Are you sure?"

"Yes," Brody responded.

"What do you see?" Reaghan asked.

"Wait for it," Brody said, then pointed to the edge of the woods by the old deck.

The adults were confused so Owen told them, "Brody has seen something coming in the woods. Don't be afraid."

As everyone's attention turned to the edge of the woods, a dark figure appeared in the shadows. Owen started to walk over to it, but Adam grabbed his shoulder.

"It's ok, Dad," Owen assured him. "It's just Jack. He's our friend."

Adam let him go, and Owen slowly walked towards the woods. The creature did not come out into the clearing, but everyone could see his form moving among the trees. Owen stepped into the shadows for a few minutes.

Reaghan started to walk over to them, and Kari warned, "Reaghan, don't get too close!"

"It's ok, Mom!" she told her. "He is my friend too! I just want to say hi."

She started walking to the woods and was followed by the rest of the kids. They hadn't seen Jack since the hunters.

The adults watched as they all disappeared into the woods, feeling a little apprehensive. They could just make out their silhouettes moving in the shadows with this very large creature. After a few minutes the thing disappeared into the deep woods, and the kids all emerged, smiling and chatting with Owen, asking what Jack had said to him.

When they got back to their parents Owen told them, "Jack thought we might be in trouble, so he came to check on us. I told him everything was ok."

"Maybe I don't have to worry about you while I'm away," Adam admitted. "It seems you can take care of yourselves."

Austin added, "And with a friend like Jack, you should have help when you need it."

"I don't know about all this," Kari confessed. "I'm not comfortable with you wearing those stones all the time."

"But Mom," Camden pleaded, "we wear them in case something needs our help! Owen can't talk to them without his stone."

"They are much stronger with them," Austin pointed out.

"I think that is why God brought us here, Aunt Kari," Owen added. "Perhaps he needed us to help protect the creatures in this wood."

"Maybe," Kari agreed, "but I don't want you keeping secrets from me anymore."

"We won't!" they said in unison.

"Is there anything else we should know?" Kristy asked.

"Well," Brody started, "you know those garden Gnomes you saw in the woods the other day?"

Kristy and Kari stared at him.

"They weren't exactly what you thought they were," Max added.

"They were real creatures," Camden confessed.

"I saw one stuck in our bush when we were cleaning up the yard," Brody went on.

"It was tangled in fishing line," Reaghan explained. "I had to cut it out of the bush, and it lost a bunch of its hair from me trying to cut it free, so I put my old dolls dress on it, to keep it warm. I named it Lilly!"

As if on cue, Lilly appeared at the edge of the woods and started chattering.

"There she is!" Brody pointed out. Everyone's gaze went back to the woods. Lilly sat at the base of a big tree. She was still dressed in one of Reaghan's doll dresses, and when she became motionless, she looked like a small statue.

"I guess that old tale about these woods having strange creatures in them is true," Kristy mused. "Maybe God does need someone to be here for them."

CHAPTER 8
Goodbye

The boys were standing at the door, saying good-bye to their Dad, again. The two weeks had flown by.

"Cheer up!" Adam told them. "I'll be back in a few weeks, and then we will have lots of time together."

Austin, Kari, Camden, and Reaghan pulled into the driveway. They got out of the car and Austin pulled his duffle bag out. Everyone gathered in the driveway while the men waited for their ride to the airport.

"Look at all the sad faces," Austin observed.

"I'm going to miss you!" Reaghan sniffled.

Austin scooped her up in his arms, "I'm going to miss you too, but I'll be back before you know it!"

She buried her head in his shoulder.

Kari said, "Daddy will only be gone a few weeks this time, and then it will almost be Christmas!"

"When I get back, we can go cut down our Christmas tree!" Austin told her.

"Can we all go together?" Owen questioned, looking at Adam.

"I think we can!" Adam assured. "I think living in the same town is going to be fun!"

"It is!" Austin agreed. "Now we can do lots of things together!"

"Maybe even a big family vacation!" Camden added.

"Let's go to the beach together!" Reaghan exclaimed.

Kristy looked at Kari, "Start looking for vacation rentals."

Kari laughed, "I'll get on it!"

Adam and Austin whispered something to each other, then Adam said, "Owen, you are the man of the house while I'm gone. Take care of your mother and brothers and be sure to listen to her. She is a wise woman."

"Camden," Austin added, "that goes for you too. You are old enough to help your mother out around the house. And be sure to look out for your little sister!" Austin took a hold of the string around Reaghan's neck that held her stone, then added, "But I have a feeling she might not need taken care of."

The kids all smiled. "Dad, maybe we need to take care of you!" Camden kidded.

There weren't two extra stones in that chest, were there?" Austin laughed.

"We will be ok," Adam promised. "You just be sure to take care of each other!"

"We will!" Reaghan agreed. "And anything else that needs our help!"

About the author

Debbie S Blankenship is a retired grandmother. Her uncle, Joe File, used to tell her children a story about a big, black, hairy thing that lived in the woods off Iron Gate Trail. Her uncle's story was the inspiration for **The Magic Stones and the Big, Black, Hairy Thing in the Woods**, her first book in the **Magic Stones** young adult reader series. She is the author of a previous novel, **Gone. . .,** an inspirational work set in the Midwest following the Rapture. Debbie resides in central Illinois with her husband, Pat. The couple has two married daughters and five grandchildren, who happen to be the main characters in these books.

55657645R20050